This book belongs to ...

_____

I Want to Be Somebody New!

by
Robert Lopshire

BEGINNER BOOKS
A Division of Random House, Inc.

For Selma, with love

Library of Congress Cataloging-in-Publication Data:

Lopshire, Robert. I want to be somebody new! SUMMARY: Tired of doing tricks in a circus, a large spotted animal decides he wants to be something different such as a mouse, an elephant, or a giraffe.
[1. Animals—Fiction.   2. Self-acceptance—Fiction.   3. Stories in rhyme]   I. Title.   PZ8.3.L862Ib   1986
[E]   85-43098   ISBN: 0-394-87616-4 (trade); 0-394-97616-9 (lib. bdg.)
Printed in Melrose Park, Illinois, U.S.A.   SP20001100APR2017   Item #: 00001-663

Once I wanted
to be in the zoo.
And that was the day
I first met you.

You said that the zoo
was not for me.

The circus, you said,

was where I should be.

And so the circus
is where I went.
I did my tricks
with spots on a tent.
I put my spots
way up in the air.
I put my spots
just everywhere!

My tricks with spots
were lots of fun.
But no more spot tricks!
I am done!

Now I want to be
somebody new.
So here's a new trick
I'll show to you!

Ready! Get set now
One, two, three...

Now look and tell me
what you see.

An elephant
is what we see!
Why, you are as big
as big can be!

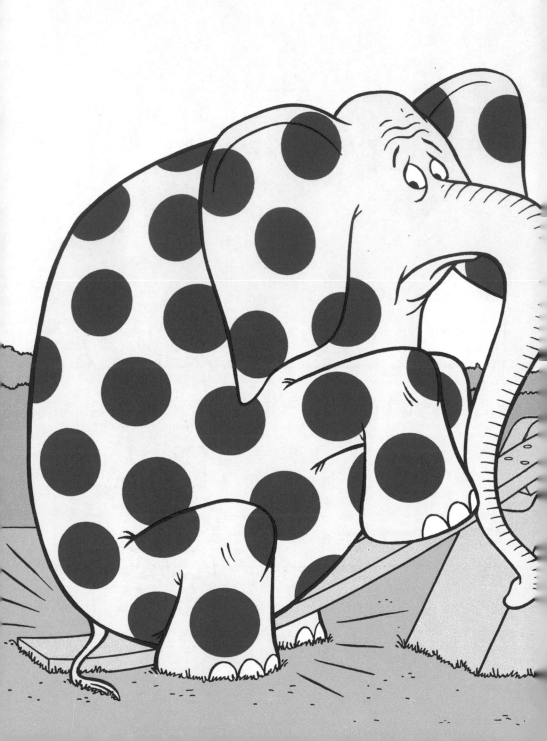

But being that big
cannot be fun.
Say! You must weigh
at least a ton!

You cannot walk
up on this fence...

or squeeze between
these circus tents.

The door of your house
is now too small.
You can't get through
that door at all!

You can't go here.
You can't go there.
You can't go
much of anywhere!

You cannot sit
in your old chair.
Your new rear end
won't fit in there.
You're very big.
You're very fat.
We do not care
for you like that.

Every word of what you say is true.

Okay. So I'll be someone new.

Ready? Get set now. One, two, three...

Now look
and tell me
what you see.

A tall giraffe
is what we see.
You are as tall
as tall can be!

But being that tall can't be any fun.
You're taller now than everyone!
Your head is now so high in the air,
it's hard to see your face up there.

And we can see
from way down here
a bird is flying in your ear!
We do not like
to see you tall.
We do not like you
tall at all!

Every word of what
you say is true.
Okay. So I'll be
someone new.
Ready? Get set now.
One, two, three...
Now look and tell me
what you see!

A mouse! A mouse!
That's what we see.
You are as small
as small can be.

Well, what do you think?
I'm asking you.
Do I look good
this way to you?

We did not like you
fat or tall.
And now you're
very much too small.
Your chair is now
too big for you.

And now your door
is too big, too!
You cannot
open up your door.
And that's not all.
There's much, much more!

A mouse cannot
go out and play.
A mouse must hide
inside all day.

And a mouse must never
make a sound.
Because that's what brings
the cats around.

There are traps put out
to catch a mouse
because no one wants one
in their house.

We did not like you
fat or tall,
and now you know
what's wrong with small!

Okay! Okay!
Okay, you two.
I'll make myself
be someone new.
Ready? Get set now.
One, two, three...
Now look and tell me
what you see!

Oh, no you don't!
You stop right there!
We like you
and we really care.

We liked you best,
a whole, whole lot,
when you were just
our old friend Spot.
So do your trick
with your one, two, three...
But show us what we want to see!

Say! You are right!
As right can be!
And it does feel best
to be just me!

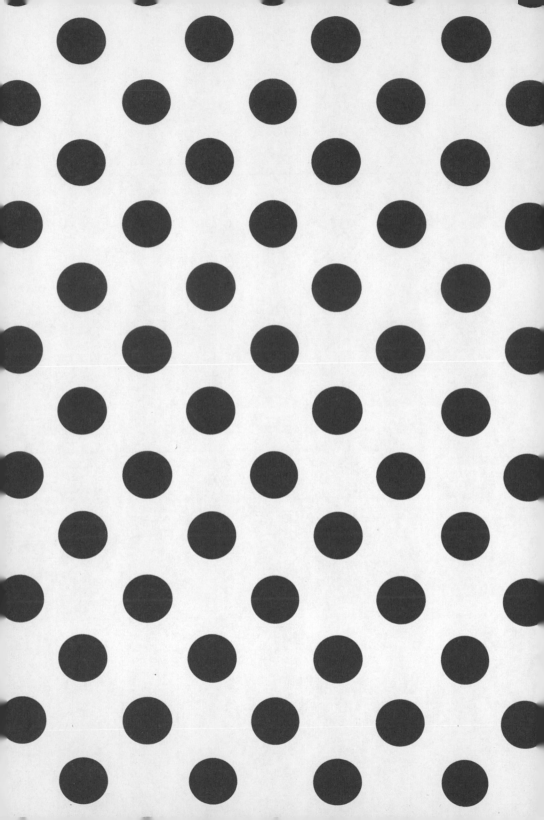